ANNIE OWNS A PONY

by JENNIFER BELL

J. A. ALLEN & CO. LTD.,
1, LOWER GROSVENOR PLACE, LONDON SW1W OEL

BRITISH LIBRARY CATALOGUING IN PUBLICATION DATA
BELL, JENNIFER
    ANNIE OWNS A PONY
    1. ENGLISH HUMOROUS STRIP CARTOONS
    I. TITLE
    741 5942
    ISBN 0-85131-524-0

PUBLISHED IN GREAT BRITAIN BY
J. A. ALLEN & COMPANY LIMITED
1, LOWER GROSVENOR PLACE,
BUCKINGHAM PALACE ROAD,
LONDON SW 1 W OEL

© JENNIFER BELL 1990
COLOUR REPRODUCTION BY
TENON & POLERT LTD,
HONG KONG.

PRINTED AND BOUND BY
DAH HUA PRINTING PRESS CO. LTD.,
HONG KONG.

ISBN 0-85131-523-2 pbk

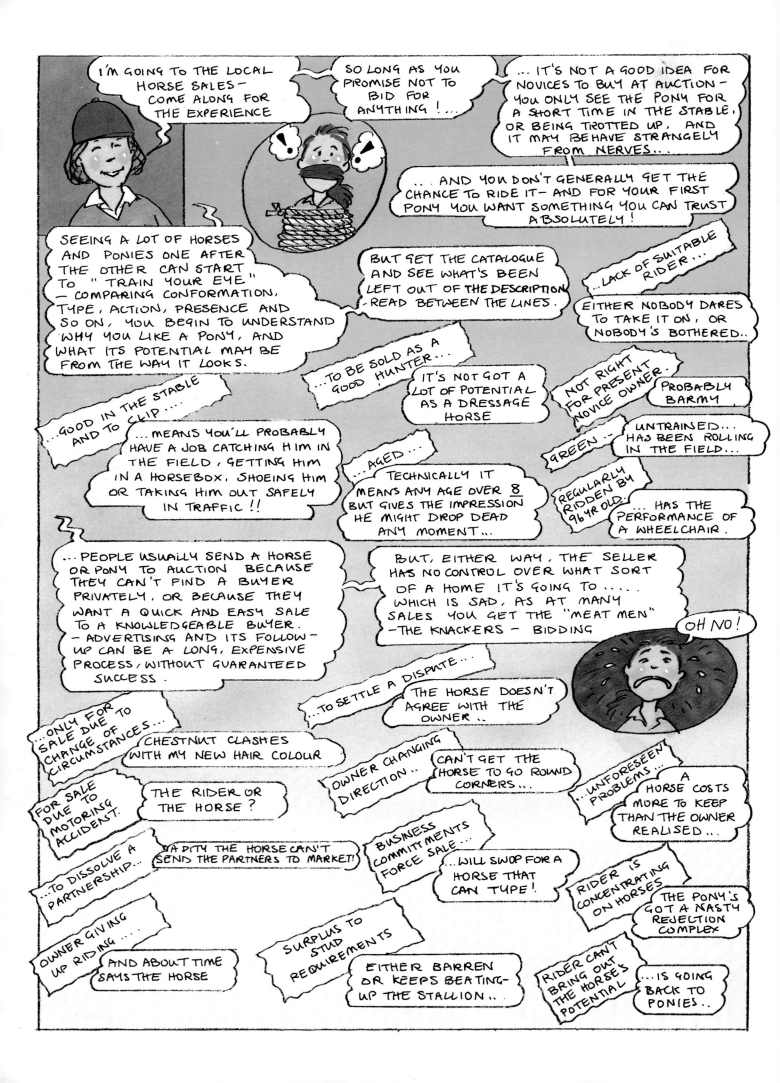

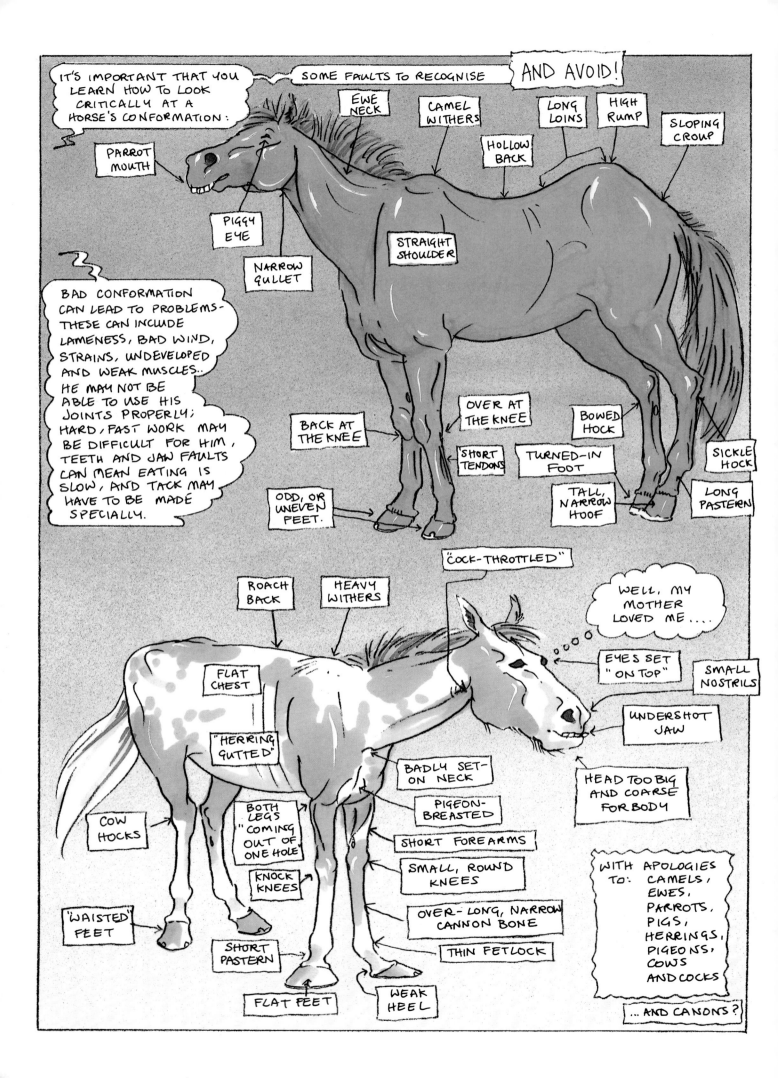

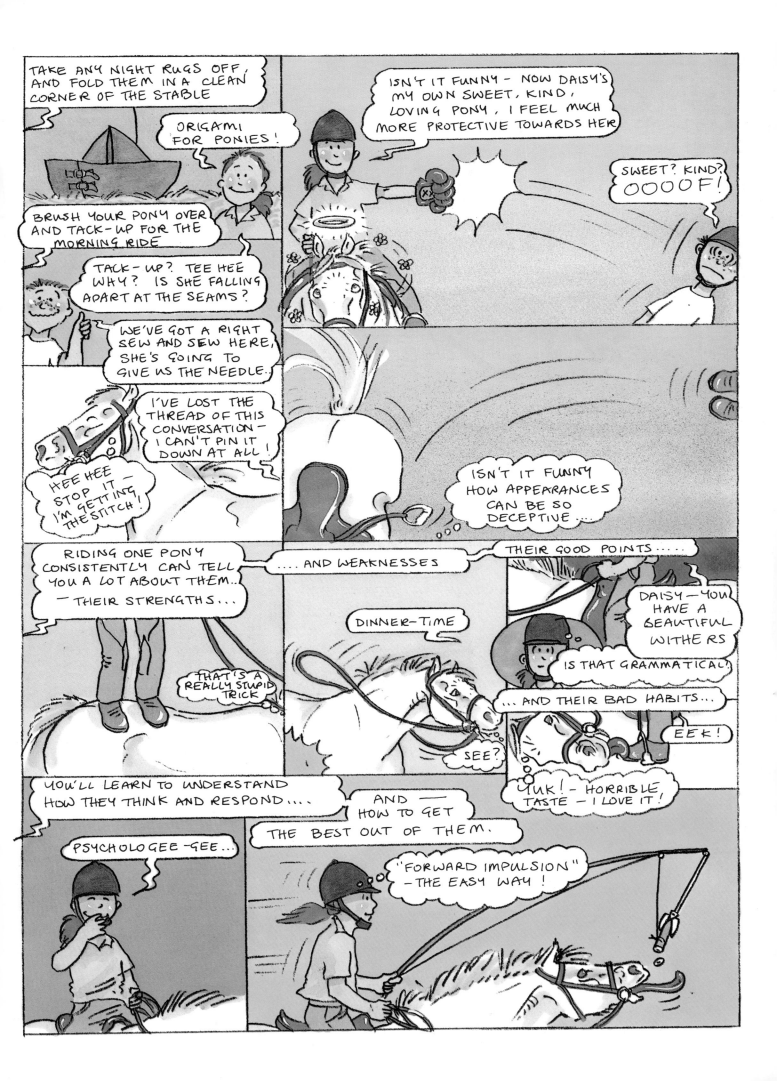

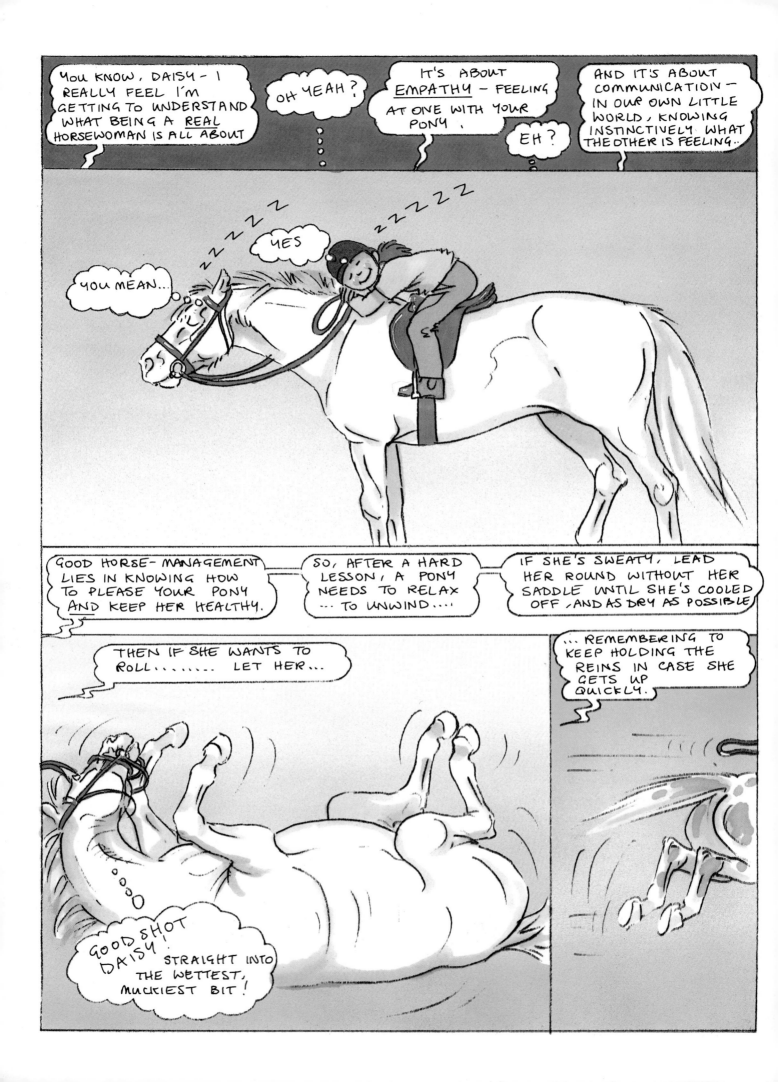

WHEN YOU'RE RIDING WITH DOUBLE REINS THEIR POSITION AT THE PONY'S END (TOP SNAFFLE, BOTTOM CURB) SHOULD BE REVERSED AT THE RIDER'S END (= TOP CURB, BOTTOM SNAFFLE)

IN THE RIDER'S HAND, THE TOP REIN SHOULD BE SEPARATED FROM THE LOWER REIN BY THE LITTLE FINGER.

THIS MEANS THAT THE FIRST REIN BROUGHT INTO PLAY BY ANY MOVEMENT OF THE RIDER'S HANDS IS ALWAYS THE MILDER SNAFFLE REIN. NEVER RIDE ON THE CURB REIN ALONE!

SOMETIMES YOU HEAR ABOUT PONIES WITH "HARD MOUTHS". THIS USUALLY MEANS THAT THE NERVES IN THE BARS OF THEIR MOUTHS HAVE BEEN DESTROYED BY RIDERS MISUSING THE BIT WITH HEAVY HANDS AND INSENSITIVE RIDING — SAWING OR JABBING — OR TOO SEVERE A BIT.

IT IS NOT A GOOD IDEA TO USE A MORE SEVERE BIT, EXCEPT WHEN YOU NEED EXTRA CONTROL TEMPORARILY FOR YOUR OWN SAFETY — CROSS-COUNTRY JUMPING FOR INSTANCE....

JUST WATCH IT... I CAN FEEL EVERY MOVEMENT YOUR HANDS MAKE.

DON'T WORRY — THEY'RE PARALYSED! I'M TOO SCARED TO MOVE A MUSCLE!

...AND DON'T KEEP CHANGING BITS EITHER — THINKING ONE DAY YOU'LL FIND THE PERFECT SOLUTION.

IF YOU'RE HAVING PROBLEMS, IT COULD WELL BE THAT THE PONY'S BASIC TRAINING IS AT FAULT, OR HE'S UNCOMFORTABLE — TAKE A LOOK AT EVERY ASPECT — INCLUDING YOUR RIDING.

BIT BETWEEN THE TEETH

HELP

I'M DOING IT MY WAY

THE BIT IS NOT ACTUALLY BETWEEN THE TEETH. THE HORSE IS PULLING STRONGLY — ENTHUSIASM TAKES PRECEDENCE OVER LISTENING TO THE RIDER (IT CAN CAUSE MUCH ANXIETY) A STRONGER BIT WILL HELP THE RIDER REGAIN CONTROL

YAH!

TRY PUTTING A RUBBER "PLATE" "TONGUE" ON THE BIT, OR USE A DROP NOSEBAND.

TONGUE OVER THE BIT.

YOUNG HORSES OFTEN DO IT IN NAUGHTINESS IT SHOULD BE DISCOURAGED BUT IF AN OLDER PONY DELIBERATELY SETS OUT TO EVADE PRESSURE ON HIS TONGUE, VITAL CONTROL MAY BE LOST HIS MOUTH MUST BE KEPT CLOSED.

BEHIND THE BIT — OVERBENDING

THE HORSE IS TRYING TO RELIEVE REAL (OR IMAGINED) PRESSURE OF THE BIT. LIGHTEN YOUR HANDS, USE LEGS AND SEAT MORE

NO! I'M NOT OVERBENDING. I'M ADMIRING MY BEAUTIFUL FEET!

ABOVE THE BIT.

FIGHTING THE BIT — OFTEN DUE TO UNCOMFORTABLE BIT, SORE MOUTH, OR THE MEMORY OF ROUGH HANDS. PUTTING A MARTINGALE ON ONLY INHIBITS THE SYMPTOMS, AND WON'T CURE THE HABIT. TRY A MILDER BIT — A RUBBER COVERED MULLEN MOUTH WILL STOP HIM CATCHING HIMSELF PAINFULLY IN THE MOUTH. BUT ALSO CHECK HIS TEETH, NOSE, EARS AND BACK.

CHANGING TO A MILDER BIT OFTEN IMPROVES A SITUATION MORE THAN TRYING A MORE SEVERE BIT. BUT THERE IS NO SUBSTITUTE FOR SCHOOLING, GOOD SCHOOLING AND REGULAR SCHOOLING

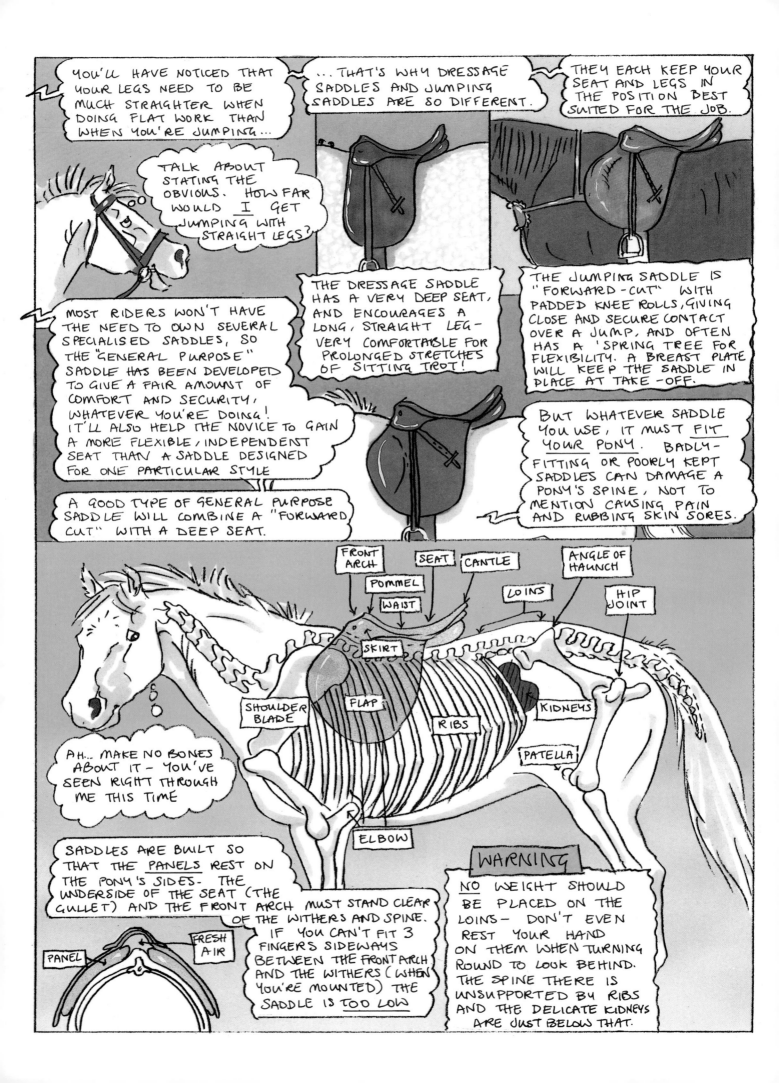

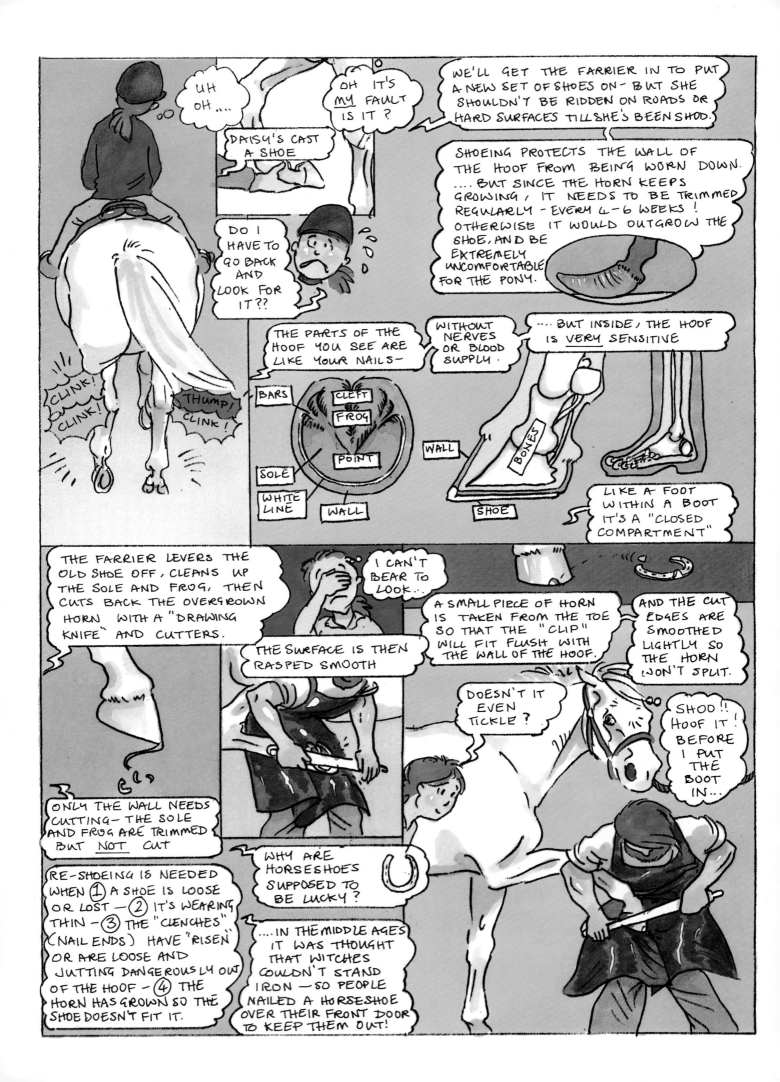